Staff

Founder and Executive Editor Meredith Allard

Deputy Editor Susan Arenstein

Senior Editor Paula Day

Contributors

Matthias Berger
Peyton Ellas
Greg Houle
Carol Zendman Howell
Warran Kalasegaran
Rebecca Kilroy
Nancy Lee
Anne Myles
Shelley Nation-Watson
Meri Parker
Paul Robinson
Kavya Shrikanth

EDITORIAL OFFICE
2654 W. Horizon Ridge Pkwy
Suite B5-364
Henderson, NV 89052

For advertising, contact:
copperfieldreview@gmail.com

For submission guidelines:
www.copperfieldreviewquarterly.com

ISSN: 1533-3736

Cover Photo Credit:
Elijah M. Henderson

www.copperfieldreviewquarterly.com
www.copperfieldreview.com.
Copperfield Press

AUTUMN 2021

COPPERFIELD REVIEW QUARTERLY

A Journal for Readers and Writers
of Historical Fiction

CONTENTS

OUR CONTRIBUTORS

Matthias Berger is originally from Germany but now makes his home in Manhattan. He is a recent MFA graduate and he is enjoying writing various types of stories, including historical fiction. He is currently working on his first novel about World War II.

Peyton Ellas writes from the foothills of California's Sierra Nevada mountains. Their work has appeared in *FiftyWordStories*, *Streetcake magazine*, *Gihon River Review*, *OnTheBus*, and elsewhere. They write gardening features for local news media and is the author of *Gardening with California Native Plants: Inland, Foothill, and Central Valley Gardens*.

Greg Houle is a writer and communications professional living in Los Angeles who enjoys telling stories about people from the past or present—real or imagined. He also happens to be the eighth great-grandson of Thomas Putnam, Jr. Follow him on Twitter @greghoule and learn more at greghoule.info. A version of Greg's story "The Putnams of Salem" first appeared in *Sundial Magazine*. It will also appear in *Dim & Flaring Lamps: A Historical Fiction Anthology of America*, which will be published in November 2021.

Carol Zendman Howell is a retired teacher and writer. She wrote "Pages" during a visit to Cambridge University using sources from the university library.

Warran Kalasegaran is the author of the novel *Lieutenant Kurosawa's Errand Boy*, which was nominated for the 2018 Singapore Book Awards Best Fiction Title and 2016 Epigram Books Fiction Prize. The novel is about a Singaporean Tamil boy who is forced to work for the Japanese military during its occupation of Singapore in the 1940s. Warran is currently working on his second novel and writing short stories. He graduated with First Class Honours in Politics with International Studies from the University of Warwick and a Master of Public Policy from the University of Tokyo. His Instagram handle is @warran. Find him online at warrankalasegaran.com.

Rebecca Kilroy is a student at Mount Holyoke College pursuing degrees in English and Spanish. She writes historical and contemporary fiction and is drawn to forgotten stories. She's been previously published in *Laurel Moon* and *The Mount Holyoke Review* where she's also served as prose editor.

Nancy Lee is a wife, mother, and poet living in Bar Harbor, Maine.

Anne Myles is Professor Emerita at the University of Northern Iowa where she specialized in early American literature. She recently received her MFA in poetry at the Vermont College of Fine Arts. Her work has appeared in the *North American Review*, *Split Rock Review*, *Whale Road Review*, *Lavender Review*, and other journals. She lives in Waterloo, Iowa.

Shelley Nation-Watson was the co-host of one of Chicago's longest-running poetry talk shows, Wordslingers, which aired on WLUW FM from Loyola University, from 1999 to 2009. She has been writing and performing poetry in the Chicago area since 1988 and has hosted several poetry venues over the years. She has been published in many poetry journals including *Wisconsin Review*, *The Dead Mule School of Southern Literature*, *The RavenPerch*, and many others. Shelley has been a teacher and counselor in Chicago for the past 26 years and holds two Masters' Degrees in Education. Shelley Nation-Watson is a citizen of the Cherokee Nation of Oklahoma and has recently begun to write about the experience of her grandmother and other members of her family as they lived through their struggles in Cherokee Nation territory in Tennessee and Alabama to the Going Snake District in Oklahoma.

Meri Parker was born in upstate New York, raised in Massachusetts and New Hampshire, and graduated from high school in Burnt Hills, NY in 2008. She studied opera for ten years but never lost her early passion for writing. She had a short story published in the *Rhythms Literary Magazine* at Schenectady County Community College in 2010 and has been working on a series of young adult fantasy novels based in a medieval world, taking inspiration from her *Dungeons & Dragons* campaigns. She now lives in a town just south of Boston, MA with her boyfriend and two goblins who have been polymorphed to look like cats. Under her real name, she is studying creative writing with a focus on fiction at SNHU.

Paul Robinson is a poet from Liverpool, England. Robinson, a former musician, is listed as a New Liverpool Poet. He graduated from Edge Hill University in 2021 with an MA in Creative Writing. Robinson's stochastic, paragenerate poetry has appeared in a number of publications, including *Monkey Kettle*, *The Ugly Tree*, *The Delinquent* (3, 4, 5, 8), *Nerve* (magazine), and *Spacesquid*. In 2011, Robinson's Genesis|Terminus project pared down the King James Bible (Oxford Standard Text, 1769) to the first and last word of every verse of every chapter of every book. The resultant work was performed at the University of Leeds School of Fine Art, History of Art and Cultural Studies; and Leeds Art Gallery in 2012. *Genesis|Terminus* was released under the Hesterglock Prote(s)xt imprint in 2021. *Spikes* is an historical record of the violence and suffering of paupers who happened to find themselves at the gates of Victorian Liverpool workhouses in 19th Century Britain. "Liverpool Workhouse" is one of the core pieces of *Spikes*.

Kavya Shrikanth is a recent graduate from the Department of Archaeology at the University of Cambridge, UK, and also holds a Bachelor's degree in History from Ashoka University, India. She has written a number of academic papers on topics of our temporal and spatial past spanning from the early humans of the Palaeolithic, the time-frozen residents of Pompeii, the swashbuckling pirates of the Atlantic, to the socio-political struggles of the colonial world. Now, as an avid reader, novice writer, and boundless enthusiast of historical fiction she hopes to channel her passion for studies of the past into the colourful world of lyrics and prose.

DEAR READERS

Welcome to my favorite time of year. Yes, I'm a fan of pumpkin spice lattes, and yes, I'm one of the crazy ones who decorates my house with colorful leaves, pumpkins, and scarecrows. Since I live in Las Vegas, Nevada where it's 110 degrees Fahrenheit in the summer, the cooler days of autumn are a blessing indeed. It's also a great time to settle in with a good book, as Nancy Lee reminds us in her wonderful piece about the particular joys of autumn reading.

We were humbled by the positive response we received from CRQ's first edition. Thank you to everyone who reached out to say they enjoyed the stories, poems, and interviews. We're thrilled that you loved them, and we think you're going to love our Autumn 2021 edition just as much.

As autumn weather arrives, I've been thinking a lot about slow living and slow writing. Those of you who are familiar with the Biblical tradition may be familiar with the idea that every seven years the land should be left to lie fallow. So how does that apply to me? I'm not a farmer so I don't have land to leave alone. Instead of a sabbatical year for the land, I'm looking forward to an internal sabbatical year.

What do I need to let lie fallow? The first thing to pop into my addled mind was letting go of my list of Great Things I want to accomplish. Like many people, I've spent most of my life working towards Great Things, some of which I've accomplished and some of which I haven't. The times when I did accomplish my goal there was always this odd silence in my head, a sort of existential *crickets*, since the accomplishment was never what I thought it was going to be.

Two days after I crossed the graduation stage in my doctoral regalia, I was taking the trash out like I normally do and I had the profound realization that my life was exactly the same as it was before I finished my Ph.D. I had wanted my Ph.D. for 24 years by that point and two days after I achieved it I realized that I was the same person I was before. It seems obvious, I know, but it was a revelation to me.

Goals themselves are wonderful things since they give us purpose, but I've set too much importance on achieving goals and not enough on the joy of the journey. Mind you, I'm not setting aside all goals for the coming year. I'll finish my current novel in early 2022. Writing a new book brings me great joy, and we should always pursue our joys.

But what would happen if I worked without any particular end in mind? What if I wrote just because I love to write? What if I wrote without any expectations? Without any ideas of what the end result should be?

What if I practiced yoga, and cooked, and wrote, and colored in my coloring books just because? What if I allowed myself time to rejuvenate without basing my happiness on any particular outcome? What would happen, do you think?

Although we're still surrounded by craziness, I hope you're able to allow yourself some rejuvenating time so that you can grow even stronger afterward.

Happy autumn, everyone. See you in January.

Meredith

Meredith Allard, Executive Editor
Copperfield Review Quarterly

WHY DO WE LOVE HISTORICAL FICTION?

In our last edition, we asked readers and contributors to define historical fiction. Now we want to know what it is about our beloved genre that keeps us reading late into the night. Why do we love historical fiction?

Nancy Lee: I love historical fiction because I can sink into the novels and be swept away. I love nothing more than a historical novel that can transport me to another time.

Matthias Berger: I love historical fiction because it gives meaning to events that seem to be disconnected from our own time but are in reality intertwined.

Mary Ressenor: There's a quote from Jewell Parker Rhodes that I completely agree with, "I love historical fiction because there's a literal truth, and there's an emotional truth, and what the fiction writer tries to create is that emotional truth." Rhodes said it perfectly, I think.

Amy Nucham: I love historical fiction that is based on real-life personalities. I love it because I get to inhabit this famous person's life, even for a little while, and see what it was like being them.

Bernadette L.: Historical fiction is practically all I read these days. I love everything about historical fiction, especially learning more about a time I'm interested in such as early American history.

Mary Anne Yarde: I think the reason why I continue to be fascinated with historical fiction is that unlike all the other genres out there, this one educates as well as entertains. When historical fiction is at its best, there is really nothing that can beat it. Where else can you walk with kings and witness some of the greatest historical events of all time? Historical fiction will always be my go-to genre. For me, it is a love affair that will never end.

Jo Beckham: My mother would read us these big books from the classic authors so I've always had a preference for books that are difficult to hold open as you read. Historical novels tend to be on the longer side and they do equally good work at transporting you to another world.

Mike Merrick: We're here in our current world but at the same time we're living another life through these characters. We can experience whichever time period we want, which is why I think historical fiction is great.

Photo credit: Alex Motoq

"WHAT A MIRACLE IT IS THAT OUT OF THESE SMALL, FLAT, RIGID SQUARES OF PAPER UNFOLDS WORLD AFTER WORLD AFTER WORLD, WORLDS THAT SING TO YOU, COMFORT AND QUIET OR EXCITE YOU. BOOKS HELP US UNDERSTAND WHO WE ARE AND HOW WE ARE TO BEHAVE. THEY SHOW US WHAT COMMUNITY AND FRIENDSHIP MEAN; THEY SHOW US HOW TO LIVE AND DIE."

~ ANNE LAMOTT

Let's talk about the joys of reading.
The joys of autumn reading.
Don't you just love it?

THE PARTICULAR JOYS OF AUTUMN READING

By Nancy Lee

I do so love the joys of autumn. Here where I live in Maine, autumn is a precious, fleeting moment of impermanence. The gorgeous foliage, the fiery reds, the welcoming oranges, the sunny yellows meld together and warm us with their glory.

If you are familiar with the Danish term *hygge*, you may already know that it means comfort or coziness. *Hygge* is a warm cup of hot chocolate when your hands are cold. It's a warm blanket in front of a fire with fresh-baked muffins by your side. It's board games with your family on a Saturday afternoon. It's pumpkins, Halloween, and, here in America, Thanksgiving. It's a chill in the air, enough to make you grab a sweater but not so much that you shiver your way home.

Like most readers, I love reading during all seasons, but there are a few reasons why autumn reading is my favorite. First of all, many new books come out in the autumn for the holiday season, so there are many wonderful new choices. Secondly, when cooler weather comes to Maine it's not as much fun to be outdoors. Yes, Maine is wonderful for us outdoorsy types, but once the summer sun begins to fade, being inside our own home is the best place of all. Finally, I love jumping into stories and leaving myself behind.

What is better than settling into a comfy chair, with a soft warm blanket, a cup of English Breakfast tea, and my favorite scones, all with a wonderful long novel to sink into? Nothing, as far as I'm concerned. This is why historical fiction is perfect for autumn. Historical novels tend to be longer so you can lose yourself in another world and another time. You can leave reality behind as you're enchanted by rich details, engaging characters, and fascinating events. You can learn about pivotal moments in history and consider how much has changed or how some things haven't changed at all. Mainly, autumn is a time for comfort reading as I reread old favorites and discover new gems.

Autumn is a season of change, when the earth prepares to hibernate so that it can burst anew in the spring. While we're waiting, wouldn't you love to grab a big book to capture your heart and mind? And wouldn't you love to be cuddled up in a warm blanket, in the light of cinnamon-scented candles, drinking tea while you're doing it?

Photo Credit: Debby Hudson

Writing Across Time
An Interview With Historical Novelist
Libbie Hawker

I first discovered Libbie Hawker's historical novels when I was searching for books specifically about Ancient Egypt. It's a time I've been fascinated with since King Tut's treasures toured the U.S. A search for Ancient Egyptian novels pointed me toward Libbie Hawker, and I'm so glad it did. Her novel *The Sekhmet Bed* is one of my all-time favorite stories set during this amazing time.

What's wonderful about Libbie is that she writes about various eras in a way that is both believable and engrossing. Want to learn more about Libbie, her writing, and her experiences publishing historical fiction? Read on.

Meredith Allard: When did you first fall in love with historical fiction?

Libbie Hawker: I've loved historical fiction since I was a young kid. I started reading very early, and I soon outgrew the kids' books that were available back in the 80s—before the golden age of kid lit, which would come along too late for me. So I just started reading my mom's books, and she'd mostly gravitated toward historical fiction herself, for whatever reason. Some of the earliest novels I can remember reading were *The Mists of Avalon* and *Clan of the Care Bear*—both of which were probably far too racy for my tender age! I think I just glossed over all the sexual stuff, though, because I didn't really understand it at that age. I was just fascinated by the evocation of a past era. It must have looked pretty funny to other people, to see me at age eight or nine lugging around a big doorstopper like *The Mists of Avalon*.

M.A.: When and why did you begin writing, and did you always write historical fiction?

L.H.: I declared at age eight that I was going to be a writer when I grew up, and fortunately my family never tried to discourage me or steer me toward a "more sensible" career. My dad was a professional artist—a painter—so careers in creative fields were just normal in my family, and totally achievable. So I was encouraged from early childhood, and I started writing my own stories then. I mostly wrote animal fantasies up until high school—novels inspired by books like *Watership Down*, which has always been one of my favorites. I hand-wrote them on notebook paper and "bound" them in three-ring binders. I'm sure my mom still has them in a box somewhere.

I didn't start writing historical fiction until high school when a truly great history teacher, Kathy Ludgate, got me excited about the past. She really made history come alive for me in the same way those old novels I'd read had brought the past to life. She got me especially interested in Ancient Egypt, and Hatshepsut in particular, telling me she thought I'd really identify with the woman who ruled Egypt as king. I did several big school projects on Hatshepsut and became a bit of a fangirl for the female pharaoh. And even though I wasn't writing about Ancient Egypt yet, I still felt a great affection for the setting and for Hatshepsut in particular.

M.A.: I've been fascinated with Ancient Egypt since I was in elementary school. How did you come to write about that period in history? What makes it a good topic for historical fiction?

L.H.: In my late 20s, I decided it was time to really get serious about starting an actual career as a writer, instead of doing it as a hobby. The moment I thought, "It's time…" I immediately thought of Hatshepsut and New Kingdom Egypt. She'd been lurking in my imagination for all those years, and I knew I could write a convincing novel about her, but when I set out to start planning my first "real" book, I found I gravitated more toward her mother, Ahmose. I was intrigued by that mural that depicts Ahmose as conceiving Hatshepsut with the god Amun, and even though I knew it was just political propaganda to bolster Hatshepsut's claim to the throne, I kept asking myself, "…but what if Ahmose actually believed it was real?" That persistent question turned into my first novel, *The Sekhmet Bed*, and I followed that one up with three novels that were actually about Hatshepsut herself.

As for what makes Ancient Egypt a good topic for historical fiction… what's not to love? It was an incredible civilization that spanned 6000 years, more or less, and was full of drama and intrigue and so much beautiful humanity. I love studying Egypt so much. There are endlessly fascinating stories to be found there. I've done ten novels set in ancient Egypt over the years—the four Hatshepsut ones (*The She-King* series), a trilogy that covers the rise and fall of Akhenaten, and a trilogy set at the end of the 25th Dynasty (*White Lotus*) when Egypt fell to an invading Persian king.

M.A.: You write different types of stories with different styles. Your novel *The Sekhmet Bed*, about Ancient Egypt, is different from your novel about Calamity Jane. How do you decide what to write? Are there different challenges with different historical eras?

L.H.: I just go where inspiration leads me. I enjoy learning about all points in history, not just ancient times, and my imagination is captured by all kinds of stories. I do find it more challenging to write about earlier eras because the historical record tends to be slimmer, so you have to infer a lot more and it's easier to get things wrong. (I prefer to have more actual history and less fiction in my historical fiction, when possible.) But I enjoy the process regardless of how recent or ancient my subjects may be.

M.A.: All authors have a different path as they seek publication. What was your journey to publication like?

L.H.: After I finished *The Sekhmet Bed*, I got an agent, and she wasn't able to sell the book after a year. She dropped me as a client and another agent at her agency picked me up, who didn't even try to sell any of my books for another year. So I dropped her. I was so frustrated by those two wasted years that I decided to self-publish...and to my surprise, *The Sekhmet Bed* very quickly found an audience and started to sell very well. Within just a few months of publishing it, the book was earning more than I was making at my day job. So I decided to commit fully to self-publishing, and I brought out several more books over the next couple of years, including the rest of the *She-King* series.

My books really struck a chord with readers, and soon I had publishers approaching me about acquiring my next book or re-releasing some of my indie books under their imprint. Self-publishing had been such a positive experience for me that I wasn't really inclined to take any of those offers, but then Lake Union Publishing came along and their offer was hard to turn down. I did agree to do some books for them while keeping my options open to continue self-publishing if I wanted to.

I've since launched a very successful pen name with Lake Union—Olivia Hawker—and some of those books have hit bestseller charts, been optioned for film/TV, etc. It has been a very positive experience, and I really love being a hybrid author. I mean a real hybrid author, who does some traditional publishing and some self-publishing. Not this "new" definition of "hybrid," which is just the old vanity-press, pay-to-play scam with a new coat of paint.

I've also expanded to work with some new publishers—this time with a good agent—and I've got my first book coming out from a Big Five imprint in February. It's called *The Prophet's Wife*, and it's about the founding of the Mormon church and all the high-stakes drama that surrounded that cultural event.

I feel that a true hybrid approach—self-publishing some books while selling others to good publishers—is the best strategy for most authors. It allows you to tap into some promotional avenues that are very difficult or impossible for authors to access on their own, while still keeping some of your copyrights entirely in your own hands. It's a powerful combination that allows you to negotiate with publishers from a place of greater strength.

M.A.: What are the joys of writing historical fiction for you?

L.H.: I just love history. It's so fun and fascinating to me; I love exploring the ways people of the past are just like people of today. Even when the set dressing changes, we're still humans, no matter where or when we are. That's an interesting truth to explore through fiction.

M.A.: What is the research process like for you?

L.H.: It's easy to get sucked into research and neglect the actual writing, so I research just enough about my setting (especially the political and social aspects—what's going on around my main character) that I can clearly see how my central character would navigate that landscape. Then I stop researching and I start writing. I pick up any smaller details, like what people in that time/place would wear or eat or how they'd get from point A to point B—as I'm writing. I'll get to a point in a scene where I need to add some kind of small detail, like describing someone's dress, for example, and I stop just long enough to Google that detail and verify that I've got it right. Then I add it to the scene and keep going. You don't need to know absolutely everything about every single aspect of people's lives during your era before you begin writing.

M.A.: Do you travel for research? If so, what role does travel play in your writing process?

L.H.: Not yet! For most of my life, I never had the money to travel. Once I finally had a few breakout books and my financial situation changed, I had to do a few expensive repairs on my house, and then I was just gearing up for some great research-related travel when the pandemic hit! Darn it. But I am looking forward to traveling in conjunction with research once the pandemic has settled down more. I'm working on a concept for a novel that will be set in Constantinople, and I'm really looking forward to visiting Istanbul to do some hands-on research.

M.A.: Which authors are your inspiration—in your writing life and/or your personal life?

L.H.: I love Hilary Mantel so much. *Wolf Hall* might be my favorite book of all time. It's not as evident in my Libbie Hawker stuff, but in my Olivia Hawker books and in my Libbie Grant stuff (*The Prophet's Wife*), I really favor a literary style, sometimes even bordering on avant-garde weirdness.

And as far as more popular historical fiction goes, I've never read a Kate Quinn book that I didn't absolutely love. I've been a Quinn fan since her earliest days. I don't understand how she just keeps knocking them out of the park, one after another. I've read some of her books several times because they're just so dang enjoyable.

M.A.: What are the particular challenges of publishing and marketing historical fiction compared to other genres?

L.H.: I don't find marketing my self-published historical fiction to be especially challenging. It goes pretty smoothly for me. But it can be infuriating to work with traditional publishers in this genre. They (and agents) are all so convinced that certain settings "won't sell," when that quite simply isn't true. Like, at all. The historical fiction audience is very broad and willing to try out all kinds of eras. Publishers are missing out on a lot of profits by believing these silly rumors that such-and-such setting is "dead" or "a hard sell." But whatever...that just leaves more money on the table for enterprising indie authors. This is why I think it's so critical for historical novelists to take a hybrid approach, self-publishing some of their work. You can scoop up a gigantic swath of readers who are waiting for publishers to put out something new and fresh, while the publishers keep chasing their own tails trying to replicate the hit they had a few books back with WWII or 19th-century frontier or the 1960s civil rights movement or whatever other hit they had.

M.A.: What advice do you have for those who want to write historical fiction?

L.H.: Do it and have fun! There's really nothing to it; it's no different from writing in any other genre. If it calls to you, then go for it!

M.A.: What else would you like readers to know?

L.H.: I have a how-to book for writers that shares my experiences (and my best advice) for establishing a career in this genre. It's called *Making It in Historical Fiction.* It's only available as an ebook since I really don't sell enough copies of it to justify all the work that goes into making a print version. Just more proof that historical fiction is a genre ripe for enterprising authors to reap a great harvest. And if you want to check out my fiction, it's all at HawkerBooks.com.

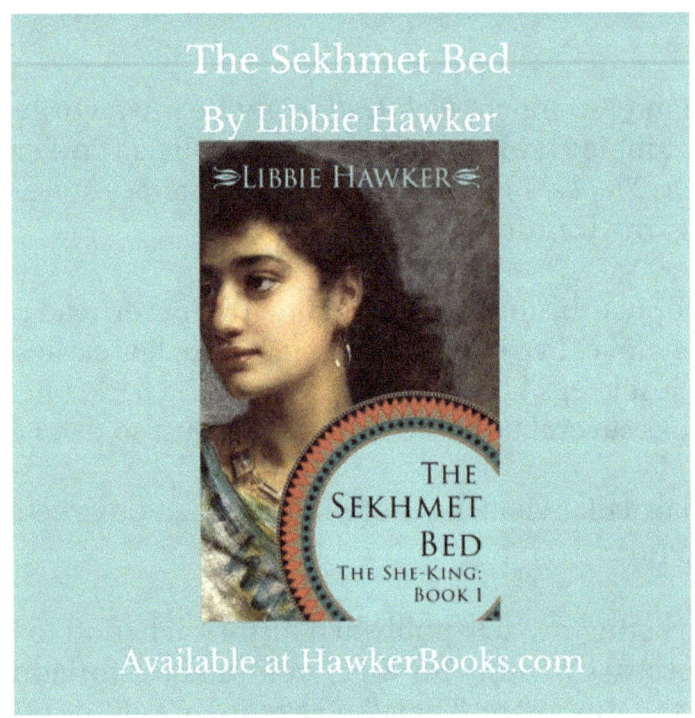

HISTORICAL FICTION

Peyton Ellas

Greg Houle

Carol Zendman Howell

Warran Kalasegaran

Rebecca Kilroy

Meri Parker

KENTUCKY

By Peyton Ellas

Father tells the family they are leaving Virginia soon, leaving the civilized world for the wilderness of Kentucky. He tells everyone in town they are going next summer. Still, creditors have come to the house. One is knocking now.

"You can't tell anyone," Mother says, standing to go to the door. They have been mending socks, a task Charlotte hates, a task they used to have a girl do, when Charlotte was younger, when Father won more often than he lost.

"I don't see why it matters," Charlotte says. "People might be glad to see us go." Charlotte joins mother at the door, socks still in her hands. The rapping at the door is louder, but still not the fist pounding that sometimes happens. Mother deals with the creditors.

"They will put your father in jail," Mother says sharply. "His debts are too great."

"At least then we wouldn't have to leave," Charlotte says.

Mother's hand flashes. A quick slap across Charlotte's cheek. Charlotte grits her teeth. Mother shakes her head once, quickly, and motions for Charlotte to get away from the door. Charlotte flings the socks to the floor and stomps to her room. She hears voices but can't make out the words. She doesn't come out for supper, and Mother doesn't bring her anything.

"If I die, she would be sorry," Charlotte thinks. She has heard stories about Kentucky. She has heard about dirt, insects, and the river flowing big and silent, ready to claim their bodies after they've been cut up, burnt, or trampled under hooves. Or ready to drown them with floods or decompose their bodies with disease and rot. She has heard that the Shawnee will kill them all: Father, Mother, herself, her nine-year-old brother Garvan, and baby Abigail.

As darkness falls, Charlotte gets into her nightshirt and crawls under the covers. Her stomach rumbles but she likes the feeling.

The next morning, Charlotte lies awake in bed, before the day begins.

Will it be different in Kentucky? Will every girl there be descended from wastrels? Why else would anyone leave the civilized world for the wilderness? How long will it last before girls there find out she has no talents or charms? Will there even be any girls her age?

As she soaps the shirts, Charlotte considers that if Father had won all those games of cards and dice, Charlotte would wear a new black velvet cap instead of a two-year-old linen cap. The day before, Phoebe and Theodosia had shown her the long riding coats and tall crowned beaver caps their fathers had sent them from Richmond. Their fathers did not gamble beyond the legal lotteries. Phoebe and Theodosia's caps had long ribbons down the back, long enough that the girls giggled as they sat on them. Theodosia, the nicer of the two, lets Charlotte try on her cap.

Charlotte pushes off the bed covers. She pulls off her shift and stands bare-skinned on the wooden plank floor of her cold room. She hasn't wanted to build a fire. Let her freeze to death. Would Father be sorry then?

Where did Father get the money to buy land in Kentucky? Did he win at a game? Why has he not paid the creditors? Father hasn't seen the house or the land he bought. What happened to the family who lived there? Father won't say.

She puts on her stay, fastens it tightly and struggles into the first of her two petticoats.

Do they gamble in Kentucky? Will it be the same? Where would they go then?

If Father were not a gambler, she could have a Black girl help her dress, as Phoebe and Theodosia do. Charlotte knows that although they pretend to be her friends, Phoebe and Theodosia pity rather than like her. Charlotte accepts this. They have no reason to admire her.

If Grandfather had not been a gambler and a thief, he would not have been sent to Virginia as an indentured man. He would have stayed in England. If Grandfather hadn't kept on gambling and thieving, Charlotte wouldn't have heard Mr. Allen say to Mr. Haught, "They's becoming like them mean whites that live on possum and can't wait to steal from you when they get the chance."

She ties on her pockets and struggles into her gown, careful not to rip it. If Father were not a gambler, Charlotte could have a new gown from Paris, instead of the one she has mended more than a dozen times.

Everything Charlotte has fits in half a trunk. Charlotte remembers necklaces, tiny treasure boxes, a wooden doll with a laced-neck dress, pairs and pairs of shoes. Those things are gone now, as is most of the furniture. Even the kitchen table has gone to pay Father's debts. Charlotte has helped Mother for weeks pack up dishes, linens, rugs, and clothing they will take with them. Everything has been loaded into the wagon that has been kept hidden in the cattle barn. Mother has said not to expect a large house in Kentucky. Where will Charlotte sleep? Will she share a bed with baby Abigail?

Charlotte has heard that in Kentucky there are no towns, no churches, no schools for Garvan. Father has told her about Daniel Boone. Phoebe said Daniel Boone was a traitor to Virginia. Something Phoebe's father told Phoebe, no doubt. Phoebe is not clever enough to have thoughts of her own.

"Better for us we're leaving," Mother says later, when Charlotte joins her downstairs. "Better for you, Charlotte. You've become too roughened, too full of your own opinions. A man does not want a wife full of her own opinions." Mother has put a biscuit, cut open and steaming, on the table for Charlotte.

"It's not my opinion that father gambles and has debts he can't pay," Charlotte says. She bites into the hot biscuit. Perhaps she will be sent back to her room. But Mother purses her lips and points at the pile of father's shirts that need washing. Charlotte has become the servant girl.

If Charlotte played at cards, would she do any better than Grandfather and Father?

There would be no way to keep up with fashions in Kentucky. Perhaps if Charlotte could bring enough ribbon, kerchiefs, and scarves she could manage. She wished she knew what to expect. She wished they had coins to exchange, the way they did in Paris and New York. Everything here is on tobacco credit. And father has none. She already tried at Hedrick's store.

She had only wanted a new comb for the curls she had managed to create on her own, without even help from Mother. Hedrick's daughter had offered to lend Charlotte one of her own combs. Charlotte had wanted to suggest rolling dice for it. But what could she give if she lost? What did she have that anyone, especially a shopkeeper's daughter, would want? And she wasn't convinced she would win. The outcome was not guaranteed even when she played dice secretly in her room against herself.

"Will Garvan gamble like Father does?" Charlotte asks mother.

"Not if I can help it," Mother says. How can Mother help it? If women are not to give their opinions, how can they have any influence?

The family is invited to a dance. Mother doesn't want to go, but Father says they must. Garvan and Abigail are left at home. At the dance, Charlotte watches Phoebe and Theodosia flirt with the young men. She wants to tell the girls that she is leaving, so she stays away from them so it won't slip out. She spies the older men playing cards in another room. She tries to enter but is barred at the door by a stern-looking man she doesn't know.

"Females are not allowed," he says. He points behind her, as if commanding a dog. Charlotte slips into a corner and watches the men for the rest of the night. She can see Father on the other side of the room.

Mother doesn't find her until dawn. "You need to make your presence known," Mother scolds as they walk home. "Decent young men will not dance with a girl who spends her time in dark corners." Father has stayed behind, still gambling. Perhaps he is winning and they won't leave after all.

"If we're leaving, what does it matter?" Charlotte asks.

"Use every opportunity to develop good habits," Mother says. She looks around them to see if anyone is within hearing.

Garvan feeds the animals on his own. Charlotte doesn't see Father until late in the evening. He smells badly, as if he has been working at hard labor. If it were warm weather, Mother would tell him to dip in the horse trough. Instead, Mother sends Charlotte and Garvan to their rooms so he can have a bath in the kitchen.

A few days later Mother wakes Charlotte before the sun rises. They climb into the wagon as the first light of dawn shows the horses' breath in the cold air. Their house is a mile away from their closest neighbors. Charlotte sits on trunks in the back of the wagon and looks out. Mother pushes baby Abigail, who is fussing and won't settle, into Charlotte's arms. The road is muddy, the sky slate-gray. It will freeze later. Charlotte is glad they are leaving before the ice.

Charlotte sees a man running after them, coming from town. It is the shopkeeper, Mr. Hedrick. Charlotte rocks Abigail and watches Mr. Hedrick. He's too fat and not used to running to catch up to them. His hat falls off and lands in the muddy wagon tracks, displaying Mr. Hedrick's wild, graying curls bouncing as he runs.

"There, there," Charlotte whispers into Abigail's ear. "You won't have any of these bad memories." Charlotte thinks of the stories she has heard of the Wilderness Road. How it is filled with bandits. "We may not even make it to Kentucky," Charlotte whispers. "Why cry about what may not happen?"

Charlotte can see Mr. Hedrick's red, puffy, angry face. Charlotte's heart beats fast against Abigail's soft warm body.

Mr. Hedrick is shaking his fist in the air. Charlotte raises her hand and waves.

THE PUTNAMS OF SALEM

By Greg Houle

In January 1692, two pre-teen children living in the household of the minister of Salem Village, Massachusetts, the Reverend Samuel Parris, began exhibiting strange behavior and claimed to be inflicted by witches. The children initially accused three women—a slave named Tituba, an impoverished itinerant named Sarah Good, and a woman who scandalized the community by marrying her indentured servant, named Sarah Osbourn—of witchcraft. Years earlier, Osbourn had upset Salem's powerful Putnam family (especially its patriarch, Thomas Putnam Jr.) when she, against the traditions of the day, claimed the land of her late husband instead of allowing it to pass down to the Putnams.

Thomas Putnam was incensed by Osbourn's actions, which hindered his ability to build upon the gleaming legacy of his father, Thomas Sr., who had been one of Salem's most prominent and wealthy citizens.

The bewitchings in early 1692 presented Thomas with an opportunity. And with some unwitting assistance from his 12-year-old daughter, Ann Putnam Jr., he was not going to let it slip away.

1.

The Lord said unto my Lord, Sit thou at my right hand, untill I make thine enemies thy footstool.
~From the sermon notebook of Samuel Parris, January 3, 1691

It came to me fully formed during that drenching, perilous ride to Salem in the middle of that raging tempest. It was a clear sign of God's mercy. I have no doubt about that. Perhaps I should not be so sure of myself but, alas, it is so. I vowed then, during that arduous journey, that if I made it to Salem, to the magistrates; if I did not fall from my horse in a soaking heap—maimed, shivering in the gloom—that it was God's will.

It wasn't about me. It was never about me. Some might not believe this but, as God is my witness, I will say it once more: none of what I am retelling was ever about only me. I engaged in these noble pursuits to strengthen our covenant with God; to ensure that our Homeland—our Fathers had risked so much to establish it—would not be eviscerated by those who so clearly wish us ruin. Why? Why do they wish us to fail in our arduous and Godly pursuit? I have no answer. That shameless itinerant and her incessant begging. That Heathen slave, always a bit too clever and conniving. And most especially, that contemptible Osborne. Who would ever stand in favor of such an unspeakably shameful hag? Good riddance!

Besides, it wasn't me alone. Others too sought justice in their own way. Edward, Hutcheson, Preston. Each made the same onerous journey to Ingersoll's, to the magistrates, each with the same, strong conviction: to cleanse Salem of the scourge that these women had been so cruelly nurturing.

Indeed, my conviction (shall I say) struck me on my journey that dark day like a lightning bolt from Zeus (if I may reference such a thing). The others—Edward, Hutcheson, Preston—had a raw and powerful vengeance as their driving force; they remained on their mounts, despite such peril, to ensure that justice be done, that witchcraft be avenged. Noble, certainly. But not exactly what I had in mind. To be sure, I sought justice too. But my justice transcended the feral and base desires of my comrades. My aims were higher-minded (if I may be so bold).

2.

I want to hide. I want to tuck myself into a cupboard or a corner or some other dark and desolate spot like a cat, wrapping my limbs around myself in a comforting cocoon to hide myself further still. But there is no comfort from my shame. No matter what I do there is no relief, save for these fleeting moments of clarity and calm. I would do anything to take away the incessant ache that encompasses my body. I know that I brought this on myself, but why can't I—despite being a sinner of sinners—be spared a moment or two of relief? I would give anything for it! Can even the most depraved of us get a reprieve from this torment? Reverend Parris—such a learned and pure servant of God; his powerful messages had compelled me to listen closely on meeting days instead drifting into my usual daze—has made clear that those of us who do not live as God had intended (by the Scriptures, of course) will surely sink our cherished community, as would a heavy anchor to a tiny vessel. Reverend Parris made it clear—clearer than any Man of God who has come to Salem before him (and there have been many in my dozen years)—that we are ALL capable of the most devious depravity. That we are ALL susceptible to the most vile temptation. Even those in his own home have been inflicted. The Reverend's home! But unfortunately the devil has saved the worst of his depravity for me.

I do take some small comfort in the fact that I am not alone in this degradation—even if it is unkind for me to say so. While others may be inflicted, I feel so very alone when I am having one of my spells: writhing, scratching my burning skin without the least bit of relief, screaming at the top of my voice and whatever other unspeakable actions I unknowingly take. If I could bury myself in a deep hole or fly away to the Heavens to make it stop I would do that and more. Anything to save my poor family from the endless shame my sinfulness has brought to them. Have I any chance of making it into the Kingdom of God? Doubtful, but one never really knows does he?

3.

My Father was a great man. Yes, everybody says this about their father. At least more say it than mean it. Their fathers and their father's father were great men, they tell us. But in my case, these words are as true as any that have been spoken. Indeed, it is prideful for me to say this but I ask: does that make it any less true? He was a Founder of this Godly land: A pillar who commanded respect from all who met him. He earned it through his pious ways and hard work, a combination of attributes that far too few possess today. And I say this with not a little bit of regret. Yet all men are sinners, and because of this, envy is never far behind most men. Many have happily done the devil's work to ensure that my Father's legacy will be cut down. But he will not be brought asunder.

4.

I do not know how I have become bewitched but it probably happened because I was not pious enough. I'm sure Reverend Parris would agree if I could ask him. I have not lived by the Scripture closely enough. I am a weak and feeble girl who allowed the devil in all his cleverness to deceive me through his devious servants. I have disgraced my family and my community and my only recourse, Father says to me in my moments of lucidity, is to renounce those who have inflicted me (the devil's helpers) to ensure that they will be brought to justice and do no further harm to our Godly community. I will do my best. Though I am not sure it will be good enough.

5.

Among his many talents, Father was knowledgeable about the land. As knowledgeable, many said and I believe, as the Heathen Indians. He had a way with the land that few other civilized men possessed—plants, herbs, medicines were all at his mercy—it was certainly a gift from God. Some—though not all—of this knowledge was passed on to me and I have used it with care and benevolence. My dear Father, God rest his soul, entrusted me to carry on his greatness in this way (if not in every way). Yes, I have disappointed him, no doubt. But I take his sacred trust in me with a seriousness that cannot be cast aside.

6.

Tituba started it but she wasn't alone. There were others. Too many for me to know about for sure. But none of that matters now because all I can do is wrap my arms and legs around my body and scream. I want to jump in the fire but Mother will not let me. Mother, I get you, let me get relief! Let me cast away the shame that I have wrought forever! I want to fly away like a bird. The Black man keeps tormenting me. Appearing over and over, haunting me as the devil himself. The yellow bird is pecking the tender skin between my fingers. Pecking and pecking and pecking and pecking.

7.

I've seen the bewitched before. We all have. The devil and his consorts are all around us, of course. We all know that. And we all stay vigilant. Like Edward, Hutcheson, Preston and others. The evil-doers tempt us and try to steer us off our beloved, Godly path of righteousness. Like those who have tried to avenge the success of my great Father by preventing me from building on his greatness for the benefit of our God-fearing community. It is sorcery that they use. They harness the unknowable power of the underworld to avenge the glory of God and his Kingdom. So I fight them (as we all must; as Edward, Hutcheson, Preston and others do) with my own cunning weapons.

8.

Father is most saddened by my infliction. When I am lucid, I see it in the creases of his face, darkly outlined by the fire light. Mother has her own troubles but Father—Oh my dear Father, so strong, so pious—grieves for the embarrassment that I have become in a way that is Godly and Good. I am so very ashamed but I know that I must try to make him proud as best as I can. How is that possible after falling so far? Yet I will do whatever my feeble and weakened mind and body allows me to do to wash this shame clean. It would be easier if Father allowed me to die. Abandoned me to my fate. But life is not meant to be easy. Instead, he patiently feeds me bread to keep my strength from waning further. He tells me (I think) that I will be well soon if I eat more. He tells me to focus my energy on those who have done this great and grievous harm to me in the name of the devil. I don't believe him when he says I will get well (how could I when I am tormented so!) but his insistence sustains me further.

9.

The bread is all that Annie will eat. Even if I wanted to give her some other sustenance, she wouldn't take it. The rye (she says in her moments of clarity) seems to give her the strength that she needs to keep going. Of course, I know (thanks to the wisdom of my Great Father and the mercy of God) that the rye has been provided to us to do much more than give nourishment. Annie is reacting well to this strange brew and if I can get the magistrates to act swiftly, her torment shall not last long.

10.

The bread gives me life, even if the life that I live is worse than death. But I want to do the work that Father asks me to do. He speaks to me so tenderly while feeding me; his words swirl around in my addled mind, mixing with the visions and colors and embers of hell that I see before me. Are they real? I will avenge the shame I have brought to my father.

11.

Annie was the only one who could do it. For a girl of twelve she is strong of mind and body. She is strong of conviction too (God bless her!) I am giving her the proper amount of rye only—as Father had shown me to do years ago—enough to elucidate her torment but not destroy her mind and body in their entirety. It is a strange and powerful skill but it is exactly what Annie needed in order to be a true servant of God and to be able to show the magistrates, the Great men of our land, the wicked deeds that these Godless women have done. I hope that they will soon see the light. Perhaps I am the witch? Could it be so that some witches are doing God's work and not the devil's? Alas, now I am trodding a blasphemous path. It is not for me to say what is the work of witches.

PAGES FROM A SEVENTEETH-CENTURY DIARY

By Carol Zendman Howell

July 10, 1631

Up betimes and to matins in the chapel. This did please the lord, my father who oft rails about our lateness in rising. Methinks it is not meet that he should make complaint of me. I am no longer a child but a lady of fifteen years and so require more time to prepare myself than doth my brawling brother who tumbles from his bed and breaks fast with sleepers in his eyes.

Much bustle in the household this day. The Duke my uncle arrives from London with his gentlemen on the morrow. The king's apartments are prepared for him. He brings with him my cousin, Lady Gwendolyn, who is said to be a gentle girl of pleasing aspect. I have had a letter by her filled with the most suitable compliments writ in as fair a hand as ever I have seen She is to stay with her maids in the apartment next mine.

Today, Master Grant the musician taught me a fair ditty from Master Will Shakespeare's play "Twelfth Night." I am to sing it on the morrow after we have et when it is usual to have musical entertainment for our guests.

Master Grant is an admirable music-maker and (tho' I would not say this except to my diary) a man of most fair parts. He plays upon the lute and the virginal with equal skill.

There arrived today from the picture-maker an admirable likeness of His late Majesty King James I such as that wrought by Master VanDyke and a fair copy thereof. It is to be hung in the Long Gallery by the Brussels tapestry where methinks it will lend much to the elegance of that hall My father hath also ordered a likeness of His Majesty King Charles and his lady, Queen Henrietta.

Today I helped Mama to prepare the fruit soups from raspberries gathered earlier by the maids. Mama wishes me to understand the art so that I may provide it when I am wed and have a household to attend. Thence to my broidery and to while away the hours with a French Romance which my father frowns upon. Since Mama delights also in this reading, he doth not forbid it. That is as well for philosophie doth not entertain Mama or me.

At six I did walk into the common hard by the house where the wenches who do keep the cows and sheep sing their pretty ballads... Alas, the cows did stray into the corn whilst they were thus occupied. Then did the maids fly like a gaggle of geese, all to my considerable merriment.

So, in excellent amusement went I to sup and thence to walk about the mazes until the light faded. When this is writ and prayers are said, I will to bed where slumber speeds the morrow.

July 11, 1617

This day hath been filled with glorious excitements. The Duke, mine uncle, and his gentlemen with Lady Gwendolyn arrived at 4 o'clock. With what joy did the company greet one another!

Mine uncle and my father might be twins so much do they resemble one the other. Except, of course, the Duke is most fashionably attired with long and curled locks and dressed in the new fashion – a flat collar and fine linen 'neath his doublet, whilst father doth persist in wearing ruff and buckram in the old style.

My cousin Gwendolyn has an air of majestie about her that cometh, I doubt not, from her close association with royalty. She is fair and taller than I. Her hair is curled and puffed most wondrously about her face. She rode not but was carried in the coach from London and was much jostled on the road. She doth not ride, as was explained to me, because she is most delicate of constitution, though she looks to me to be well enough.

For me my Cousin Gwendolyn had caused to be made a mirror with a mat of stumpwork wrought by her own hand. How lovely it is and how well it will look upon my Flanders chest. And more to co. Lady Helen who waits upon my cousin pulled from her cappe case a length of damas for my lady mother and a pair of broidered gloves for me.

After the party rested and was refreshed thereby, my cousin and I walked about the garden and through the pleached avenue whilst she told me of her life at court. She is betrothed to the Earl of Sunderland. He is a gentleman of high birth and royal connexion. She reports that tho' elderly, near forty, he is still quite spirited. The couple are to be wed in London November next when the dower is arranged. Lady Gwendolyn this day hath done me the honor of requesting that I attend her at the ceremony. The prospect is most pleasing to me.

My cousin and I the ladies are to join the gentlemen in the long gallery where the musicians played most sweetly. At the request of my father, I sang several of the songs taught me by Master Grant to the apparent delight of the assembled company. The Duke took special note of what he called my dulcet tones. It is a wonder that I sang so well as that scamp, my brother, did contort his face most awfully to disconcert me. I shall complain to Mama about it.

Then the lady Gwendolyn was asked to sing which she did most prettily. 'Twas the music of Lawes married to the as yet unpublished verse of Milton's Comus. The company received it well. I noted that Master Grant gazed upon her brazenly as she performed, and thereafter made special compliment. I cannot think why my father allowed it. Nor did Lady Gwendolyn cast down her eyes – and she is betrothed!

After a late meal of sack posset and cold meats, the company dispersed, I to write in my diary and so to bed.

July 15, 1631

Have not writ in this diary for several days as the entertainment of the visitors from London hath prevented me.

We have been practicing for the masque that is to be presented the Saturday next. There is much ado over the costumes and the scenery. The whole is most cleverly devised by Sir Phillip Brooke and doth bespeak his talent in such enterprises. He has caused to be created a goodly ship upon a rolling sea, a most excellent illusion thereof.

On Thursday eve the neighboring gentry and some others attended a feast and a ball thereafter. So many were the guests that the most were served in the great hall and some even in the steward's parlor – all on bords and benches. We et in the chamber at the drawing table and sat us on buffet stools with wroughte Kyschynes.

The Duke expressed within our hearing his displeasure with young Sir Harry Marworth, a gentleman in his service. That fellow is wont to sit among the grooms and pages rather than in that estate which belongeth to his degree. My cousin observed to me that such is the humor of many young men today. London, she says, is full of like examples. She attributes it to the parliamentary spirit that is abroad. I find it a most curious circumstance.

The feast was sumptuous and lasted severall hours. Mutton a la Doode was served to us along with beef, chickens, ducks, and a swan dressed most artfully (though I like not the meat.) Besides roasted meats there were meat pies, pasties, vegetables and sallett of lettuce, cucumber and chicory – all with much wine and pleasant bonhomie.

After these courses we did repair to the withdrawing room. Therein a banquet of sweets was set out, a fine array of quince tarts, Banbury cake, marzipan, gingerbread and I know not what else. The gentlemen rose with us tho' it is their custom to remain at table for serious discussions unsuitable for ladies.

Lady Gwendolyn's attire conformed to the very latest London Fashion as described by our neigbour, Lady Pamela Forbisher who has lately been to the city. My cousin's hair was curled in lovelocks for the occasion with yellows bows and ribbands thereon. Her gown rose high at the waist and low about the neck with a georgette of lawn all trimmed in lace. Her stomacher was of yellow tuft taffety, the skirt of yellow silk, all tucked up and held fast with yellow bows of a deeper hue to show her petticoats of finest lawn – all most delicate and well-contrived tho' I own that yellow becomes not her complexion.

I am irked to note that my cousin is provided with fine lawn for all occasions while I, at times, must be content with scotch cloth. I wonder that Mama hath not observed this.

The dancing did commence at ten that evening. There were measures, galliards, courrantos and lavattos, those being most performed at court. I had many partners from the company but none so graceful as Sir Harry Marworth. That gentleman hath a quick wit and a pretty air about him.

The musicians played with spirit, except for Master Grant who seemed in heavy humour and stared the while at Lady Gwendolyn with eyes not like those of a moon calf.

It was after three when, the night being much spent, the local company parted. The rest of us hastened to retire and I to my bed without a word recorded in this diary.

On the Friday the company slept late and I fear the chaplain said his matins alone. I was wakened by my mischievous brother. The jacknapes was hurling stones against my window, a thing he has been forbidden to do. If my father hears of it he will be beaten. If not, I shall for certain box the scallywag's ears myself.

During the morning my father and mine uncle rode about the estate while we ladies sat with our broidery in the drawing room or strolled about the gardens. Some of the gentleman walked there, too. Others entertained themselves in the shovelboard parlor.

After the midday meal we practiced again the masque, and, my part being done, I walked into the garden thinking to discover Lady Gwendolyn therein. As I neared the grove, I beheld a scene that gave me pause. I espied my cousin in the close embrace of Master Grant, the music master. Thinking to rescue Lady Gwendolyn, but knowing not if she welcomed those advances, I proceeded with much racket to give fair warning. At the sound of my approach the couple sprang apart. My cousin's cheeks were fiery red while his were white as in death. We spake not one to another. Then did Master Grant fly from the grove whilst I supported the trembling Lady Gwendolyn back to the house.

I was sore troubled to know what course to take in this misadventure. Should I report the matter to my father or to the Duke? If all were made known, then what of my cousin's honour and her reputation? What of her betrothal? Would the Earl cast her aside and she become a fallen woman? Would there be no wedding? Would I then not have the honour of attending her in London? And if I said naught of the affair, would my cousin continue on this disastrous course and so bring shame upon her family?

Forthwith in troubled spirit, I hied me to the chapel to pray for guidance in this grievous matter. There, in a curious way, my prayers were answered. For dear Mama who daily brings fresh posies to stand upon the altar against the reredounse entered and discovered me. So amazed was she to find me in an attitude of prayer that she questioned me most closely. Despite misgivings, I poured forth the woeful tale. When I had given the account, she enjoined me, nay, made me swear to speak no more of the affair. And so foresworn, I went to my chamber with my heart considerably lighter.

I did not see Lady Gwendolyn again that day. She being ill-disposed did not join the party but supped with Lady Helen in her apartment.

July 16, 1631

No further news of note today but to report the masque is well-prepared and all await tomorrow's festivities.

One circumstance is worthy of report. My uncle, the Duke, most generously did bestow a goodly sum of money on the musician, Master Grant, so that he may further his musicianship by study abroad. The fortunate fellow hesitated not but made haste to pack and this very day bade us all farewell. My cousin was not there at his departure. He bowed to me in a courtly manner and I wished him God speed. I believe he was grateful for my friendly parting and for his new good fortune.

Thus is my diary brought to date and all circumstances full reported. Now I to my prayers and so to bed with pleasurable expectation for the morrow.

THE COAT

By Warran Kalasegaran

He pulled his coat about him tighter against the cold French winter as he wandered about the outdoor market. It was a coat made for a British soldier, much too big for his own frame, and thus hung loosely. Whenever he forgot to hold onto it, the wind rushed in and touched his body and made him shiver. The safety pins were not strong enough either.

Everything around him was strange and alien. The white mountains in the distance where he returned to fight at an altitude and cold and dryness that were alien to him. The first time he had seen snow it had been soaked red in blood and black in gunpowder. A once possibly beautiful landscape plundered by rows of trenches and barbed wire, artillery shells firing overhead, soldiers shooting each other to death, corpses stuck in the ground like irretrievable fossils until the next ceasefire. Back in India he longed for rain as a reprieve from the heat. Here, the rain made him curl up in shivers, hoping for battle just to heat his body up. The attempts to send the soldiers food and sweets similar to what could be found in India only made him miss home even more.

The village where he went to spend leave was strange too. The cobbled stone streets, the thatched houses, the inns with strange signs and strong beers to boost soldiers' morale before they marched back to death. The alphabet was like English, but he did not know what they said in French. However, the French treated the Indian soldiers like they were equals, allowing them to billet in their houses, changing their bedsheets, attempting to talk to them, without paying heed to race or caste. The French had cheered him and the other Indian soldiers when they arrived in Marseille, and later when they came to this village before moving out in commercial red buses to the frontlines. They thanked them in a strange language that sounded like an owl's hoots, giving them little pins for protecting them against the Germans.

A woman in the village came to him and touched his coat, felt it crush between her hands where she should have gripped his arm. "This is too big for you," she said.

"You speak English?" he asked.

"Oui." She laughed, realising she had reverted to French. "Yes."

She was just a little shorter than him. Her brown hair was tied in a bun behind her head. Her eyes were the colour of a dirty green river, tired but twinkling with the necessary fight against the bleakness of the times. Her button nose tilted upward also spoke of resistance. Her smile was genuine and kind, even as she beckoned him to her clothes shop to make a sale. He followed her anyway. He enjoyed the brief human connection in this strange landscape.

At her shop, she found a coat the same khaki colour as his, and held it out for him to try. Obliging, he took the rifle off his back and set it against the wall. He had to learn to use that new model on the frontline, the first time he fired it also the first time he fought in France. She seemed to consider the weapon, as if not having noticed it properly before, not realising a killer was in her shop. But she shrugged it aside. He took off his own coat and laid it over a stool. She helped him try on the new coat and stepped back to take a look. An equality of treatment he would not have received from a white woman in India. He was surprised by the snugness of it at the chest and waist and arms. Something that fit. She smiled approvingly and pointed to a tall mirror. "Take a look."

"Why do you speak English?" he asked as he stood in front of the mirror. It was indeed a good fit.

"My father was English," she said. "You are from India?"

"Yes," he said. "Do you know about it?"

She shook her head.

"Imagine if the whole of Europe was a country. Then you have India."

"Which part of Europe will you be from?"

He scrunched his face as he thought about it. He only knew France, or more specifically, the trenches in the white mountains in France and the strange village nearby where he spent his leave. "The part of Europe that is in the south, where it is hot, there are lots of good crops to grow, and people like to sing and dance. In my village, we would run with bulls."

"Spain," she said immediately, pointing at him to see if she got it right.

He shook his head. "I have not been."

"Neither have I. It's over there." She pointed at the wall – west.

They laughed. It was an odd moment of humanity in this desolate, barren part of the world. It was a shame it took place on the last day of his leave. He would have liked to see more of this woman but didn't know if he would make it back for his next leave. Sadly, he took off the coat as well. "I am sorry, but I don't have enough money for this." He extended the coat to her. "I didn't mean to waste your time."

She shook her head. Coming closer, she pressed the coat to his chest. She seemed comfortable with him, safe. She behaved like she knew him. "Keep it," she said. "You can leave me your old coat instead."

He rose taller at the kindness. "Thank you. What is your name?"

"Marie. What is yours?"

"Raja."

* * *

Four months later, he returned to the village. He had survived just for another chance to see Marie again, to feel that moment of humanity and life that made all the death and fear and hollowness worth it. The coat was already blackened by the time he returned to the village. Black from the dirt of gunfire, the blood of his closest friend who died in his arms and asked him to keep his Sikh kara bangle, Raja's own blood where he had been shot. But the coat had kept him warm, kept him company, and gave him something to look forward to, to stay alive for. She smiled in recognition when she saw him at the shop. "I knew you would come back," she said.

"How?"

Marie touched a finger to the black patch by his shoulder, as if imagining the pull of the trigger by the German soldier across the frontline, the crippling pain as he fell back into his trench just as he had been about to crawl out, another charge in vain. Some distance from him, he faintly saw the Punjabi Muslim unit yelling "Allahu Akbar" as they climbed out of their own trenches, only for several to fall back inside as a torrent of bullets ripped through them. His friend struggled to take off his coat and clothes to get the bullet out, frequently distracted and ducking down as the shells landed around them in violent blasts.

"Don't lose the coat," Raja remembered telling his friend in Tamil before he blanked out.

Marie stopped, realising she was very close, their breaths mingling. She pulled apart. "It is a lucky coat," she said with an affirmative nod.

He took out the money from his pocket. He had saved enough of his meagre pay by then. "I wanted to pay you for it."

Marie laughed at the money and he frowned. Was it too little? She went to her own desk and took out money. "I should pay you," she said. "Your coat fetched a far better price. I got the better end of the deal."

"Let us split it then," he said.

"How?"

Her home was one of the thatched cottages he had first found strange. It was a small house and she let him in when he arrived for dinner. The fire was burning, and he took off the coat and hung it by the door. She was wearing a long blue dress, stockings, and blue shoes; and her hair fell over her shoulders. He was still in uniform. He had cleaned his boots before coming over and felt less awkward about not taking them off. She led him to the dining room down the hall, where the table was already set with what the coat's profits could afford: roasted duck, boiled potatoes, peas, and carrots. She had lit candles. There were two empty glasses. She smiled at him warmly, pleased that he was impressed with the set-up. "Do you like champagne?"

"I have never tried it." He had only had beer since he arrived. And once he had tried a bitter wine.

She looked aghast. She picked up the light-coloured bottle on the table and looked at it with disappointment. "This is very bad champagne and it might spoil your taste for it. But we don't have much else. I thought I should pick out something special for a special friend."

She watched closely as he took a sip. The liquid tasted gassy and strong and filling. He was thirsty and gulped down the glass. She looked amused and poured him another glass, as well as one for herself. "Try to appreciate it slowly," she said. Marie kept her eyes on him as she sipped her own champagne delicately, and something charged up his spine and forced him to look away. There was some boisterous cheering outside. The curtains were drawn and Marie pulled them apart a little to see several British soldiers walking past, drunk on beers from the inn, heading to a brothel at the end of the village. She closed the curtain quickly and he understood. There was no point drawing attention. "Please sit," she said.

The duck smelled funny. Supplies must have been running out, he thought, as he took a ginger bite, expecting something expired. Immediately, he knew it wasn't duck. He had never had it before, but it must have been beef.

"Do you like it?" she asked, looking worriedly at him.

He forced a smile, and made to chew and swallow. "Very much."

She smiled happily at this and tucked into her food, them sitting by the corner of the table, beside each other, elbows touching every now and then, keeping his back charged upright. She had put in effort to cook and he didn't want to disappoint her. He would eat it all. "Why did you join the war?" she asked.

He had been hurtling through the beef, leaving the potatoes and vegetables untouched, as if to get through to the other side so he could finally relax and enjoy the rest of dinner. But at her question, he put down his fork and knife down and sat back. "I guess the war came to me."

"The English," she said.

"The Germans bombed the city I was living in – Madras."

"In Spain."

"In Spain." He nodded. "They attacked from the sea, what we call the Bay of Bengal. They killed my wife, Shanti, and my daughter, Nandini."

"You wanted revenge?"

"Yes." He fought hard to keep the emotion from his face.

"Did you find it?"

He looked at her, this pretty, kind woman who had offered him a coat. Her eyes were curious, wanting to know the answer, but showing an interest in him. Her presence made him feel at peace, allowed the emotions to dissipate on their own. He realised that she was the only thing no longer strange about this strange village and its strange mountains and strange weather, far from the family and city he knew. But home would not be the same when he returned either. He read the nationalist papers the British censors tried to block them from reading. He knew the mood back home was changing. The same censors who would scrub out any reference in his letters if he wrote about spending an evening with a white woman, although he had no one to write letters to as well. It would not be the same Madras, or India, when he went back. If he went back. "No," he said. "But I'm not looking for it anymore."

"What are you looking for then?" she asked.

"A piece of home."

She put a hand on his, and he felt hot at the touch. "There is no home anymore," she said. "Are you ok with that?" Her dirty river eyes met his dark brown ones and he wondered if he understood her correctly. He didn't even know how to respond.

"Is that why you don't keep memories?" he asked. Her eyes followed his around the empty walls. There wasn't even a clock in her home, as if the war had paused time.

"You can't lose what you don't hold onto," she said.

He turned his hand up to hold hers, their fingers slowly fitting into each other's, seeking solace in each other. She leaned forward and kissed him. The beef, vegetables, and champagne unfinished, she stood up and led him upstairs.

They spent whatever time he was away from the trenches together, his brother soldiers not knowing where he disappeared to, but suspecting he had found himself a prostitute he liked. "Don't think you are the only one," they warned and guffawed whenever he took off. "She will stay with you until an officer comes along. The red pepper pays better than the black." That was how they referred to white soldiers: red peppers. He paid his comrades no mind. Teasing was the price of brotherhood. They would just as much save his life as they would make fun of it. But Marie's home had become a sanctuary. One that he started departing reluctantly to return to the interminable trenches of this interminable war, carrying only her coat with him.

Except that one day the war did end. And they had time to retrieve the irretrievable corpses and bury the dead and think of the future they had survived to anticipate. His officers made plans to return the soldiers to India. But there was nothing left for him in Madras. His parents were dead. His family was killed. Even his small business destroyed. In the French village, there was familiarity. There was her. A piece of home.

It was not difficult to disappear. All he needed to do one night was to wake up and walk. He left behind his rifle, for he had no desire to kill anymore. He kept only a rucksack and her coat for company and fast-marched back to the village. He could follow the mountains for direction now. They were no longer strange, but a guidebook he could read. Just like he could read the stars from the Madras coast. The weather no longer cold, but cool and snug. The language more familiar as he had picked up words over time. He had enough money to change clothes on the way, a better disguise, but he still kept the coat. It was her coat.

Finally, after several days, he reached the village. It was the same day as the outdoor markets he had first met her amidst. But her shop was closed. The people milling about looked at him strangely. They had been happy to see him once, but now they seemed to wonder why he was still here. He paid them no mind. He made for her house and saw her standing outside, holding a bouquet of irises. She had a baby bump and he stopped and wondered at that. But then a man's hand came into the picture and it felt the bump tenderly. She looked queasy at his touch and he made forward in anger. But then the man kissed her on the lips and she kissed him back, beaming as he stood next to her and put an arm around her waist. They were taking a photo in front of her house. A French soldier. He was wearing Raja's old coat.

THE DEATH CART

By Rebecca Kilroy

October 6, 1918

The girl could not stop the death cart. The fever would not allow it. Nor would the neighbors who had piled into her room, drawn by her mother's wails. They pressed the girl into the bed while they peeled her brother from her side. They wrapped him in someone's grandmother's quilt and his own mother's front curtains. They bound all this in cord so that the death cart, jostling over the cobbles, would not unravel him. The mother stared on with eyes as white and empty as the sky.

All the while, the girl whimpered and clawed and kicked against the ones who held her. Later, they would swear her cheeks glowed with hell's fire.

How could they take her brother away? How? Why? Why when his skin was still warm under her touch? Still flush with the life she felt sure burrowed there?

She did not know that it was her own feverish heat that had spilled into him as she clutched him to her, all night, and had become trapped beneath his skin. The neighbors tried to explain but she clawed at them like a thing possessed. Her nails tore her pillow open and white feathers exploded over the neighbors, the mother, and the bundle. They held her down until she fell into a furious sleep.

The death cart passed with the rasp of bones and was gone.

* * *

The young priest had never been sure there was a God until he discovered he was the victim of a vengeful one. He knew his sins: vanity, pride, his hands. The priest had always been too proud of his hands, smooth and unstained as Scripture pages. Especially when clasped in prayer, he felt the swelling sight of their beauty.

He'd joined the priesthood to avoid the Great War brewing across the sea and spare his hands. It was really exchanging one noble sacrifice for another, he'd told himself. A clerical collar was as good as a uniform. Both channeled a higher cause and stopped people stuffing white feathers into your hands- the coward's symbol. There was no need to put himself through a war. His perfect hands twisted and recoiled at the thought. The trenches thick with dirt that drove itself into you. Cracked skin digging through oozing mud. The profane intermission between dust and dust as putrefying bodies anointed themselves with puss. No, no, he would spare himself.

How God must be laughing now.

He jabbed his spade into a thick soup of consecrated mud and dug. The blisters on his palms burst open again. No one had offered him bandages, much less gloves. They'd issued him a weapon and ordered him into a trench. The men who'd started the work sneered at them: the soft-handed seminary students, cowards all of them, finally foisted off their pedestals.

The men shouted new commandments of their trade, in mocking, half-blasphemies. Thou shalt cram as many as bodies possible into each pit. Thou shalt toss them in like logs into a stove. Thou shalt not waste everyone's time giving last rites to every stiff and sinner on the carts. The priest still muttered blessings under his breath as he worked, tumbling over the words until they lost all meaning. It was the only way to avoid thinking, especially about God.

It was important, above all else, that they never stop. Idle hands did the Devil's work and apparently, they did it in hell. But no, hell would not reek with so much mortality.

He hoisted himself out of the trench and crossed to the death cart to begin unloading. The first bundle off was small enough to carry on his own. The revulsion of this fact that he might have felt a day ago had flattened to a sinful relief that it was so light. He slung it over his shoulder and sloughed towards the mouth of the trench.

Something white fell on the ground in front of him. A snowflake? In October? He bent closer. Not snow. This would never melt. It was a feather, white and soft as his hands once were. The kind of token they used to hand to shirkers on the streets. By some miracle one had dropped, directly from Heaven no doubt, into his path.

The priest threw back his head and howled with laughter.

Other hands pulled him out of the dirt, ran over his skin, pressed themselves to his face. They felt half the fires of hell burning under his cheeks.

"Another one's caught the flu," the voices said. "Send him to bed. He's no use to us now."

And that was when the young priest learned his God was merciful too.

* * *

The small bundle he'd dropped lay where it fell, the cool mud of the churchyard soaking through the stranger's quilt and chasing any heat away, if heat there was left in the still grey skin.

The boy hadn't died looking like himself. In the short time the fever had danced through his body, it had stolen the clear eyes his mother recognized, the round cheeks his grandmother pinched, the tight grip that held his sister's hand as they walked. There was no pretending he was anything other than he was. How many boys slept alone, in an un-revered churchyard, with a quilt covering their faces?

And if he had been asleep, the bells would've woken him.

In those days, the bells were witness and mourner and prophet. They rang without stopping for breath. But they would stop someday. And the people would sigh for the silence and then they would sigh for the song.

THE DIARIES OF CATERINA BRISANI, MERCHANT WIFE OF FLORENCE

By Meri Parker

1494-1502

6 April 1494

Today was Mother's funeral, buried with my youngest sister who never took a breath. I clutched Angela's hand on the way to the Cathedral of Santa Maria del Fiore, where the Requiem Mass was to be held. Her chubby fingers were sweaty in the unseasonably hot weather. I relish in this sisterly closeness, though she is nine years younger. Our brothers, Piero and Giovanni, have run ahead with Father - at seven and nine, they are too old to be coddled by a girl, making me appreciate Angela's small hand in mine all the more.

Mother's body had been in the cathedral since last night and had spent the time receiving prayer from the bishop who would read the Mass. Father had gone last night as well, but as the eldest, I was left home to look after the younger children. The Mass was traditional, and the bishop called us to prayer:

"Requiem æternam dona eis. Domine."

"Et lux perpetua luceat eis," we responded.

"Requiescant in pace."

"Amen."

16 May 1494

Father has hidden us away as King Charles VIII of France leads his troops to Florence's walls. Giovanni, Piero, Angela, and I are locked in an interior room until our leaders can understand why Charles has led his troops into Italy. We must protect our lives and innocence, lest these men relieve their urges on our persons. Angela is by my side, but Piero and Giovanni are complaining at the door that they aren't allowed outside to see the king's horses.

Later that day

Father has just come in to check on us, to ensure we are safe. I'm sure the stories he's told us of the time after Cosimo's death, when the streets ran red with the blood of conspirators, run through his mind at this army that has marched to our gates. He's been with the other high-ranking merchants arguing how best to handle this siege. Many of them are hoping to appease Charles, as they do not wish to go to war, but there are some holdouts in the Settanta, particularly our leader, Lorenzo de Medici. I can understand his hesitation, as it seems Charles' demand is the exile of the Medici family. I hope it does not come to this, as I cannot imagine our beautiful city without Lorenzo's guiding hand, but Father says that Lorenzo will eventually yield to protect us, as a good leader should.

12 November 1498

After months of instability, Florence has finally restored a form of functional government with the restoration of our magistrate families to power.

I should clarify, of course. Back in May, Savonarola, our leader installed after Lorenzo accepted Charles' terms of exile, was executed by order of the Church. As a man who had attacked the Medici rule and declared that their exile had been an act of God, the Church turning against him in the final years of his life seems a cruel justice. He, of course, brought it upon himself, as he allied himself with the French pope rather than our true pope in Rome. He ignored the summons of our true pope, and was prohibited from giving any of his sermons, which were always meant to strike fear in our hearts. When Charles came to our gates, Savonarola preached that he was an instrument of divine wrath, sent to cleanse us all of our sins, beginning with the exile of the greatest sinner of all - Lorenzo - and claimed that Charles' arrival was as the flood of Genesis.

Perhaps I am harsh, but I do not believe any man should compare God's divine acts to those of a mortal king. His heresy was justly punished, even in its irony. Father did not want me to attend the execution, as he feels that women should not see such things - and I am a woman now, as Father has begun negotiations for my hand - but I could not stay away as this tyrant swung from the gallows.

I've said that Father has begun negotiations for my hand. While I am happy to fulfill my duties, it breaks my heart for Angela. While we were once the wealthiest family in Florence, second only to the Medici, Father says earlier losses mean that only one daughter can marry, as no one but the church would accept such a paltry dowry as what will be left for Angela. She has been talking of marriage to a merchant lord, despite still being a child, but she is only meant for marriage to our Savior.

I pray that Giovanni's apprenticeship in finance brings our family back to a more favorable state so that any daughters he fathers will be able to wed, whether to a man or to the faith. Piero is still too young to apprentice, but he shows promise in his schooling in philosophy and mathematics, though Father says he despairs at his literature. But is literature truly important to becoming a merchant as Father intends? I suppose that's something that, as a woman, I will never truly know.

2 July 1501

Today was my wedding day. I'm taking a moment to compose my thoughts, as I have retreated to Angela's cell in the cloister, where she was placed upon my betrothal to Signor Antonio Brisani, a man nearly twenty years my senior. Father had apprenticed Antonio before I was born, when he was younger than Piero, and reconnected with him during his last voyage to the Ottomans. The last time the two had seen one another was 16 years ago, at Antonio's marriage to his first wife, Lucia. Father had not considered him for me, and would not have still if not for this chance meeting, when he learned that Lucia had died as Mother had, birthing a child - though this child, a boy named Riccardo, still lives. He is precious, younger than Angela, and his chubby cheeks remind me of Piero when he was that age, and he toddled on his little legs bringing the rings down the aisle.

I have been told what is expected of me tonight. I confess, I'm scared. Antonio is handsome enough, and I trust Father to not sell me to someone who would cause me intentional harm, but I remember how tired Mother was when she died. Will that be my fate, too?

Later that day

I tried reading a book Angela keeps in her cell. *The Book of Margery Kempe*, it's called, to see if I could take my mind off what's to come. It was of no help at all. It spoke of the suffering women experience during childbirth. I'd known Mother to be sick when she was with child, but will it be thus for me as well? I still fear for what is to come tonight, and for what will come as a result in later months.

Even later

I have finally emerged from the cell after reading more of Margery's book. She is not comforting but is honest. And her experiences in the marriage and birthing beds brought her closer to our Savior, which I view as a paramount importance. Perhaps this will not be so bad.

Father spoke to me as well. I could see his discomfort - normally it would be a mother having this discussion with her daughter, but we had to make do. Father says that above all, I must maintain a friendship with Antonio, for a strong friendship will make a strong marriage. I asked Father some more about

Antonio, but he said that I should ask my husband.

It's strange writing those words. My husband. I am married.

13 September 1501

A great artist has arrived in Florence - or, rather, has returned once again now that Savonarola is gone. Michelangelo fled near the same time as the Medici family, but has returned to complete a commission given to him to complete a statue begun in Donatello's day. It's said to be a statue of David, though only his feet were freed from the marble. It shall stand on the peak of our cathedral, and shall show all of Italy - nay, the world - that, though we are smaller than those who may go against us, we are still able to bring them down with our wisdom and strategy. What better message is there to send from the city of art?

My first two months as Antonio's wife have gone well enough, though I still awaken some mornings expecting to be back in my bed at Father's house, with Angela bringing me her hornbook to help her practice the Lord's prayer. The nuns have taken over her education, and I am to focus on bringing up Riccardo to prepare him for the apprenticeship he will have when he turns thirteen. It passes the time, though Riccardo is abysmal at his letters. He is only five, though, so there is time to learn before he begins his real schooling. Antonio is soon to begin a trade journey. As he travels, he has plans to leave me in charge of the household, a role I intend to uphold with the decorum expected of a noble merchant's wife. He will be departing in four weeks' time and will be gone for four months. He's asked me to pray for him daily, and I shall. Despite our difference in ages, he has treated me well since we married.

I am beginning to feel ill, so I will retire until our evening meal.

10 September 1502

Our magistrates have seen fit to elect Piero Soderini to the role of gonfaloniere - a lifetime position - in an attempt to stabilize our city after Savonarola. He is another French supporter, though, so I doubt he will last long in power. Like Savonarola, the pope will call him to Rome, he will refuse to go, and then he will be executed I should not write of such things. Imagine if Antonio were to get a hold of this diary! My words would bring him shame. I'm sure that Signor Soderini will rule aptly. Surely my doubts are from interrupted sleep as the twins fuss from hunger in the night. Their wet nurse is competent, coming at Antonio's recommendation from her experience with Riccardo, but sometimes I feel like I should be caring for them myself, even though it is not my place. My time with them will come when it is time to teach them their letters and their feminine duties. I hope to be around for them longer than Mother was for me.

Tomorrow I am taking lunch with my dear friend Lisa del Giocondo. Her husband is commissioning a portrait for her by a genius, Leonardo da Vinci, as an anniversary gift. Perhaps Antonio will commission one of me when we've been married as long as Lisa has been. I believe that providing such artists with our patronage will allow them to create more great works, and it is refreshing to have a friend who feels the same way.

1509-1519

25 October 1509

I take back all the foul words I have said about Signor Soderini. Our war with Pisa has reached its end, with Florence emerging as the victor and claiming the Pisan territories for ourselves. His appointee for the oversight of Florentine defense and war is a young man by the name of Niccolo Machiavelli, who, surprisingly, looks with favor upon Savonarola's preaching, but there is no denying his strategic mind. It is such a relief to know that we are once again at peace.

12 May 1513

I cannot believe I am writing these words. The Medici family has returned to Florence, and Signor Soderini has been exiled. Father had told me that the Medicis had been exiled to Seville, in Spain, after Charles laid siege to our city nearly twenty years ago - has it really been so long? Lorenzo was unhappy with his displacement but did not have the power to make a triumphant return. But his son - Giovanni - could make this return. With our last pope, God rest his soul, taking his seat in the hall of our Most Holy Father, Giovanni could put forth his bid for the highest office of the Church, and he has won it, becoming Pope Leo X. His nephew, Lorenzo, now controls our republic.

Despite our standing army, installed by Signor Soderini, Medici's Sevillian army made short work of our defenses, though much of the bloodshed was avoided by Soderini's quick surrender.

As a child, I'd hoped for Lorenzo's return, for I did not believe the demand for his exile was just. But now, I cannot justify Signor Soderini's exile any more than I could Lorenzo's all those years ago. Despite my initial misgivings, he was a wise, fair ruler, and did not deserve to be driven out of Florence to Dubrovnik.

Perhaps someday, like the Medicis before him, he will find a way back into our city.

My brother, Giovanni, is pleased by the Medici return, however. He plans to find employment with them as a banker, now that his apprenticeship is complete. I pray for his success and his safety.

22 July 1519

I write in place of my mother, Caterina Brisani, who passed away this past week at 37 years. Plague swept through our fair city, sickening rich and poor alike. My twin sister, Francesca, and my sweet baby sister, Anastasia, also perished. Father and Agnolo survived, by the grace of God, though I fear Agnolo is much weakened, and Father's business is bordering on ruin. Had my dowry not already been paid to the del Giocondo family, I would be bound for the cloister with my aunt, Angela. Fortunately, Father was able to borrow enough from my uncle, Giovanni, a banker in service to our Prince, Guilio, to ensure I wouldn't become a spinster or a nun. My heart is broken at our family's losses, as I know it was Mother's greatest wish to see us travel down our paths in life, but it was simply not to be. I thank God that her words will live on.

Caterina's ever-faithful daughter,

Gemma Brisani

POETRY

Anne Myles

Shelley Nation-Watson

Paul Robinson

Kavya Shrikanth

MARY DYER, QUAKER, WRITES FROM PRISON

By Anne Myles

1. Boston jail, October 26, 1659, under sentence of death

Whereas they insist you're guilty of your own death,
your own blood. You deny it; there's always a woman
they blame from the beginning. Came voluntarily,

they say. You think we're only hounded by our will;
the way's to give it up, feel God command, that surge
of waves beating against the hull, riding up and down

like the act of generation. Wasn't it He that brought you,
hand like a midwife pressing on your back, moving you
out of and into Boston, aiming your set, attentive face

past the church door, boundary stone, prison gate?
They thought a hanging death could quail you. You know
your way is trust in the face of fear, and your body

witnessing before power. You've felt your softness
stepping across the line, your bones rattling the cage of law.
Long ago you learned you were a story. Two days now

makes time enough to tell it for yourself, *for this very end*
He has preserved my life until now. Burying old shame, what
you sought was perfection. And the one you lost

you've found, now multiplied, such brethren and sisters,
the holy people and seed which the Lord hath blessed.
For five decades you've been traveling towards this,

now merest iron stands between, where you can hold
yourself close, lean a cheek against it, pass a tender epistle,
speak and hear the vaulting syntax of salvation.

How it flows to bode the fate of Boston! *Woe is me for you.*
The Lord will overturn you by his righteous judgments—
as you grip the quill with dirty fingers, reflecting

that in heaven she must be proud; the warning she gave
you give now in her stead. You are a publisher of truth,
you're one they can't not know, Marie Dire back again,

but what is she? You have no life separate from your people;
you're a saint; you're a neck to break; you're Esther
before King Ahasuerus; you're the breathing Word.

2. Boston jail, October 28, 1659

You raise your voices over drum tattoo and crowd, three
Friends to the gallows. You flush with joyous certainty:
for this you were born. First Robinson, then Stephenson speak

and swing. Now you ascend to noose and handkerchief—
now you will say—but a voice cries "Stop! She is reprieved."
Sun smites your eyes; your numb feet can't find the rungs.

Back again to jail, two days allowed to leave the colony.
The Lord's wrath hovers, but your sacrifice is bound
within the play of politics. You grasp you are a counter

shifted on the board. They hope it will suffice, terror and threat:
better not to hang a woman, not one with husband wealthy
if a heretic. *I can do no less than once more to warn you,*

you write, but can hear it's words. *I rather choose to die
than live, as from you.* So it seems you have a will left after all.
The pulse beats in your throat. Here you are alone,

wrenched back to the terrible self, the woman of strangest fate—
Mistress Dyer of London, Boston, Portsmouth, Newport.
Where's God's hand now, who permits you to obey them,

stunned as you are, heartbroken? Fallen leaves drift
outside the window; bodies are tossed in a pit; the root
inside your heart beds deep, to wait for a new spring.

DURING AND AFTER THE REMOVAL

By Shelley Nation-Watson

The Hanging
Jacob West (October 11, 1843)

There are whispers in my ear
chains dragging along my feet
I am surrounded by ghosts that laugh
I am being judged by haints
I am screaming inside my brain, numb
Trying to figure out what went wrong.

Listening to murmurs that won't remain silent
trying to shut it down,
I focus on the rope ahead of me
Hands tied behind
Trousers tightened 'bout my knees and
ankles lest shit spews from
Pants while I dangle and squirm from
The drop.
Sweat forms on my skin
Each drop of liquid shows I am living
If only a few minutes longer.

The hangman faces me down
Our eyes meet and I see hate bounce back
A look of malice as if I did the killing
That the knife belonged to me and not my son.
Hanging for holding a man down
I am asked if I have any last words
I have none
a black hood fitted over my head
At 160 pounds I'm given an 8 feet drop
I gasp as the rope is pulled over my head
The tightening of the noose
The shuffling of feet behind me
In a few seconds I'll cease to exist
I won't be aware of my own breath
The beating of my heart,
The buzzing in my brain,
The sound of silence disappearing.

Shoot Out
Franklin Pierce West (*December 17, 1886*)

There are words pulled from fire
Powerful heat bound together
Energy rising smoke filling
Every crevice that surrounds
Trees, grass, the plastic chair
Set uncomfortably close to the flames
Smoke is rising mind expanding
Thoughts pervading knowledge invading

I shot Sam Starr
Sam breakin' into a local post office
My brother John C. shot 'im from right off his horse
Horse died, Sam got hit
I got all the blame
Went to get help for Sam's shot up arm
left deputies to watch over.
Sam got away, but turned 'imself in,
fearin' Hangin' Judge Parker.
So, he waited for his trial and up come
Lucy Surrant's Christmas party.
I stood out back soakin' up the flames
hands soakin' up the heat over the fire
six-shooter at my hip
Belle told Sam that I was out back
Eggin' 'im on
"Bet do sumpin' 'bout him killin' my horse!"
Storming through the house,
Sam confronted me
Words became polluted
entangled within the flames
Turning into ashes of anger
Both reached for our hips
Explosion became blood an' both of us
Dropped near the fire
Both dead within an instant
I heard the embers cry.

The Camps
(1839)

It begins with my neighbor's screams.
I had ignored the men with guns
military soldiers in and out.
John Ross said he'd save us.
Children away playing
Threats encroaching
Door flung open and I am
Dragged out the open door
Clutching the frying pan in my
Right hand
My neighbor's screams become my own
Angry faces, spittle on my cheek
Bare feet gather soil between my toes
For miles I am forced to walk
My skirts drag the ground, collect seeds
Bunched in the folds.
From town to town
We stumble, I recognize
Homes like mine being looted or burned
Clothing, utensils, children's toys filling bags
To be dragged onto wagons
On the other side of the forest,
I am pushed towards a shack
Inside I see neighbors,
Cousins, strangers
This will be our new home
For 4 months
We will starve together
We will share disease and death
Open sores and vomit
We will pray to our creator
We will mourn together
We will wish the ground to open up
And rescue us from this torture
Where are my children?
I call to my husband in my head
He is silent.

LIVERPOOL WORKHOUSE

By Paul Robinson

Tankard perches on Victoria
the Workhouse towering below Mount and Hill
Stephenson's locomotive Rockets inter-city

So you and your neighbours have
children
to be made comfortable out of
our pockets

Supersized families
living off benefits

Ruth is buffeted by lustrate night gales,
bellowing coaled steam from submerged cuttings
Hitchcock Reilly's guilded scholars
opposite purgatory's eastern ravine
Broadhurst presides over unseen screams
thunderbussing through Rectors' Fields
cast and re-cast
sulphur burns *crawlin' ferlies*

Pressed on to Liverpool
Beattie to Bicknell to Bray to Beattie
Cora matrons the crestfallen
Carr's bones feel the rath of Agnes

Hugh tightropes the Circus of the Night Asylum
shedding his rags for course junk after tumbling with Soldier
Little Johnny Hughes begs on Gill St
lodged in Addison's hot entry
Yonge disembarks at King's abandoned   by Alabama
ensconced in Huddersfield, captive in Sheffield's amphitheatre

Epileptics below able women's yard
locking wards beside children's scalp & itch
outside the pauper's waiting room shed
overseer, clerk, collector, surveyor
opposite end to airing ground

Zuchthäusern upons

its power of segregation

decoupled from the Leper

a new purification Carrying morality's

madness

Lazarus and Agonal Cheyne-Stoke the bastiles
Warburton enacts governors to slice the dead
raised brows in Surgeon's Book Club scan
ornate windows between cabs
      and manure

Resurrectionists mel-an-choly 1832's slim-pickings
channelling rustification of bodies now recessed
in taphonomic performance

if I didn't have my family, I think I would be dead or in jail

this poor boy received punishment [...] the blows of which was heard in the old men's bedroom

the agonizing cries of innocents writhing under the lash, heard from within

denizens Knoxs aristocratic neighbourhoods
inmates hierarchy terrortorialised spaces

who has the right to speak and in what way?

THE LADY OF VINCENNES

By Kavya Shrikanth

Part I

The river watched with silent eye
Twelve men in uniform rush by
A nun, a priest, a lawyer; wry
All carried forth to testify
To remote Vincennes.
Unbeknownst to all who sleep
That early Paris morning deep
A reaper lurks among the sheep
Watching as the cortège, bleak
Marched to death, the spy.

A final cadence from the tower
Sang the rhythm of the hour
Echoing through fog thick cover
As the dawning sun did cower
Hiding from Vincennes.
For tales have told to be a wary
Of dancing siren, dancing fairy
Treading soft and light and airy
Whispering her forlorn story
The dancer and the spy.

Though she is known in all the land
For silken charms she waves in hand
For striking poses in her stand
For holding gazes and command
All the way to Vincennes.
Does she never stray illusion?
Or transform in her seclusion?
Under cloak, away from vision
Hide dark secrets in elusion?
Deceiving all, the spy.

Part II

Her mystic arts were not her own
But borrowed from a sacred cove
Far in the east, an island home
With husband, child; yet all alone
As she was in Vincennes.
In childhood too, she was a-stray
Her mother dead, father estranged
By eighteen she was whisked away
A Dutchman with an army pay,
Oblivious to the spy.

Once she learnt the world of wonder
And found escape from her blunder
Let her marriage tear asunder
Left her children and her plunder
On her path to Vincennes.
There she developed anew
Changed her name new colours drew
Found her graceful footing; grew
Travelled round the world she knew
As dancer or as spy?

But she a woman, on her own,
Voyaging through a war-torn zone
Suspicions shown while rumours groaned
Was there more to her unknown?
Uncertain till Vincennes.
The French approached her in their plight
Asked if she their foes could sight
To find reserves they had to fight
But soon saw her in German light
And cast her as a spy.

Part III

Now I your wistful voyeur see
Your spirit dance so gracefully
The words of French and British be
Your mournful tales and fantasy
Oh, fateful Vincennes.
Your songs of old are seldom told
I hear a distant beat but hold,
For this is not your ode exposed
'Tis just the ghost of tales retold
In your image as a spy.

An empty field before my eye
A wooden post between the rye
Your only shroud the darkened sky
Gravely waiting for you to die
In remote Vincennes.
A velvet coat of fur lined leather
A pompous hat attached with feathers
To the waiting post they tether
As you stood without a tremor
They accused you as a spy.

And you bid your blindfold withdrawn
Firing squad set, twelve rifles drawn
You blew a kiss to all thereon
Twelve shots were fired and the dawn
Crept slowly into Vincennes.
And graceful as your act could be
You bowed in death to take your leave
I could not save you from decree
And even now you are not free
Mata Hari, the spy.

NEED HELP MARKETING YOUR HISTORICAL NOVEL? THE COFFEE POT BOOK CLUB IS HERE

We always think that writing historical fiction is the hard part, and it certainly can be. But what do you do after you've finished your historical novel?

If you've written historical fiction and you'd like to get more eyeballs on your book, you're in luck because The Coffee Pot Book Club, run by mother-daughter team Mary Anne Yarde and Ellie Yarde, can help.

Meredith Allard: When did you first fall in love with historical fiction? Why are you fascinated by historical fiction?

Mary Anne Yarde: I fell in love with history and mythology at an early age. I was the child who dragged the encyclopaedia of history down from the shelf so that I could look at the pictures while wishing I could read the text!

One of my favourite novels as a child was Anne Sewell's unforgettable *Black Beauty*. *Black Beauty* satisfied my insatiable appetite for everything equestrian, but I also really enjoyed reading about the historical backdrop that this novel depicted. When I was thirteen, I discovered Bernard Cornwell. After devouring *Sharpe's Rifles*, I was desperate for the next book in the series, but unfortunately, our household budget did not include books and the library did not have them! One of my dearest friend's father came to the rescue, for he had the whole Sharpe series (up till then) and he gave the books to me. I was in book heaven, and I devoured the books one by one!

Ellie Yarde: My first experience with historical fiction was when I was eleven and I discovered *The Roman Mysteries* series by Caroline Lawrence. I remember being drawn into the ancient world and found myself wondering what it would have been like to live in a time so different. Historical fiction can do something that no other genre can achieve; it can bring back people long dead and worlds all but forgotten, simply using the written word.

M.A.: Who are your favorite historical novelists and your favorite historical novels?

M.A.Y.: That is a really difficult question for me to answer as I have so many favourite authors and books!

E.Y.: I have never had a particular answer for my favourite book, or favourite author, as I have always loved so many different books that I feel like I would be betraying one by picking the other!

M.A.: What inspired you to start The Coffee Pot Book Club?

M.A.Y.: I founded The Coffee Pot Book Club (formally Myths, Legends, Books, and Coffee Pots) in 2015. My goal was to create a platform that would help historical fiction, historical romance, and historical fantasy authors promote their books and find that sometimes elusive audience. The Coffee Pot Book Club soon became the place for readers to meet new authors (both traditionally published and independently) and discover their fabulous books.

M.A.: What do you find to be the joys and challenges of promoting or marketing historical fiction?

M.A.Y.: I really enjoy working with authors to help market their novels. The satisfaction one feels when I have helped a novel move up the Amazon ranking and get that exciting orange bestselling Amazon badge is addictive. I think my most memorable marketing achievement was helping an author fulfil her dream of becoming a USA Today bestselling author.

E.Y.: Historical fiction is a genre that some people love and some people do not enjoy at all. Helping to spread the word about a book, and letting those people who love the genre know about the book, is something magical. You know that you have helped someone find their new favourite book.

M.A.: What is The Coffee Pot Book Club and how can it benefit readers and writers of historical fiction?

M.A.Y.: The Coffee Pot Book Club promotes historical fiction, historical romance, and historical fantasy, both traditionally and independently published. There are some real gems in the indie world, and I want to get those books in front of readers who might not necessarily have heard of the author.

M.A.: Is there anything else you would like our readers to know about your work?

M.A.Y.: The Coffee Pot Book Club offers promotional opportunities for everyone's budget and we work closely with authors to help them decide which promotion would work best for them and their books. If you'd like to learn more, visit https://www.coffeepotbookclub.com.

The Coffee Pot Book Club

What's New

in

Historical Fiction?

By Matthias Berger

Every autumn there is always a wonderful new array of books to choose from. This autumn is no different, especially for fans of historical fiction. What are some of the newer releases in historical fiction avid readers should keep their eyes out for?

Harlem Shuffle by Colson Whitehead. This latest novel from the author of the award-winning *The Underground Railroad* does it again with the story of a heist in Harlem in the 1960s.

The Lincoln Highway by Amor Towles. Towles' latest novel takes place in 1954 when eighteen-year-old Emmett Watson leaves a juvenile detention center. Emmett and his eight-year-old brother head to California to start a new life but they end up on the east coast in New York City.

China by Edward Rutherfurd. If you're a fan of Rutherfurd's epic novels, *China* will not disappoint. *China* begins in 1839 and continues through the present day and works well as a showcase for China's fascinating history.

The Stolen Lady by Laura Morelli. Morelli's wonderful novel spans five centuries, from Florence in 1479 through France in 1939. It combines art, history, and mystery as da Vinci's most famous painting comes into play.

Go Tell the Bees That I Am Gone by Diana Gabaldon. Fans of the *Outlander* series will be pleased to know that *Bees*, the 9th book in the series, will be available in November 2021.

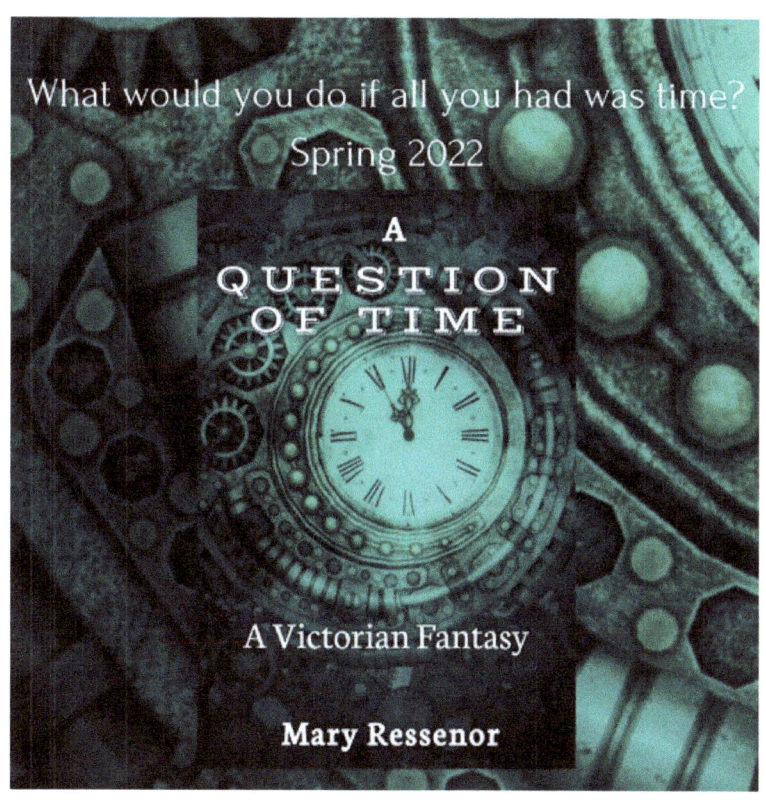

What would you do if all you had was time?

Spring 2022

A
QUESTION
OF TIME

A Victorian Fantasy

Mary Ressenor

PAINTING THE PAST:
A GUIDE FOR WRITING HISTORICAL FICTION

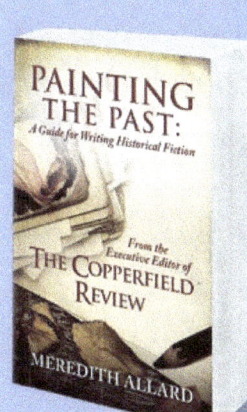

"This book is a must-have for any writer thinking about working in this genre." ~San Francisco Book Review

Available at all major online retailers.

www.ingramcontent.com/pod-product-compliance
Lightning Source LLC
Chambersburg PA
CBHW082055090726
47909CB00010B/3046